W9-ASD-480

THE BOXCAR CHILDREN®

THE SEA TURTLE MYSTERY

Time to Read® is an early reader program designed to guide children to literacy success regardless of age or grade level. The program's three levels correspond to stages of reading readiness, making book selection straightforward, and assuring that when it's time for a child to read, the right book is waiting.

Level 1 — Beginning to Read
- Large, simple type
- Basic vocabulary
- Word repetition
- Strong illustration support

Level 2 — Reading with Help
- Short sentences
- Engaging stories
- Simple dialogue
- Illustration support

Level 3 — Reading Independently
- Longer sentences
- Harder words
- Short paragraphs
- Increased story complexity

Library of Congress Cataloging-in-Publication data is on file with the publisher.

First published in the United States of America
in 2022 by Albert Whitman & Company
ISBN 978-0-8075-0677-6 (hardcover)
ISBN 978-0-8075-0676-9 (ebook)

Printed in China
10 9 8 7 6 5 4 3 2 1 HH 26 25 24 23 22 21

Cover and interior art by Liz Brizzi

Visit The Boxcar Children® online at www.boxcarchildren.com.
For more information about Albert Whitman & Company,
visit our website at www.albertwhitman.com.

THE BOXCAR CHILDREN®

THE SEA TURTLE MYSTERY

Based on the book by
Gertrude Chandler Warner

Albert Whitman & Company
Chicago, Illinois

"Something is in the water!"
said Benny.
"Something big!"
The Aldens were in Texas.
Jessie knew Benny was worried
about swimming in the ocean.
"Don't worry," she told him.
"I'm sure it's just seaweed."
But Benny was right.
Something *was* in the water!

“A sea turtle!” said Violet.
She knew sea turtles lived in
the water around Texas.
She didn’t think she’d get to
see one.
“Turtles can be that big?”
asked Benny.
Henry chuckled.
“People say everything is big
in Texas.
What better way to start our
adventure?”

Henry, Jessie, Violet, and Benny
loved adventures.
The children had once lived in
a boxcar in the forest.
They had all kinds of
adventures in the boxcar.

Then Grandfather found them.
Now they had a real home.
And they still found all kinds of adventures.

"Stay back!" a man called.
"That animal is endangered!"
Benny jumped away.
"It's dangerous?"
The man shook his head.
"Not dangerous, *endangered*."
Jessie explained, "That means
there aren't very many of them."

“That’s right,” the man said.
“We don’t need children bothering it.”
The man pointed to his badge.
“Leave this to someone official.”

Just then a woman arrived.
She wore a uniform with a
gold badge.
Her name was Ranger Thakur.
"She looks even more *official*,"
Benny said to Violet.
"I will take it from here, Mr.
Chatman," the woman said.
"We just got here," Violet said.
"Is everything okay?"
The ranger smiled and nodded.
"Actually, you came at the
perfect time.
This turtle is laying its eggs!"

The turtle spread sand over
its eggs and crawled away.
“Turtles can’t stay at their nests,
so they hide the eggs in the sand.
We need to move them to safety.”
“Can we help?” Henry asked.
Mr. Chatman grunted.
“Help? You’re just children.”

The ranger held up a tiny egg.
“Remember, Mr. Chatman,”
she said, “even small things can
make a *big* difference.”
She turned to the Aldens.
“Come by the ranger station
tomorrow.”

The next day, Grandfather dropped the children off at the ranger station.
The Aldens learned all about helping sea turtles.
"We need to find the nests quickly," Ranger Thakur explained, "or else an animal might dig them up.
That's where the Turtle Patrol comes in."
At the end of the day, she gave each Alden a badge.
"Now we all look *official*," said Benny.

To celebrate, the Aldens went
to a restaurant.
Inside they saw a familiar face.
“Mr. Chatman, what are you
doing here?” Jessie asked.
“Aren’t you on the Turtle
Patrol?” added Benny.
“Don’t be silly,” said Mr.
Chatman.
“I only do that when I’m not
working.
This is my restaurant.”
He led them to a table by
a big fish tank.
Violet looked inside.

"I wonder where the fish are," she said.
Benny crossed his arms.
"I wonder why Mr. Chatman is so mean."

After supper the children went
to their campsite on the beach.
It had been a long day.
But as Violet was going to sleep,
she saw two figures on the beach:
one person and one very big dog.

What were they doing out so late?
She remembered what the ranger said about animals digging up nests.
She hoped the turtle eggs would be okay.

In the morning, the children went back to the ranger station.
“It’s very windy,” said Ranger Thakur.
“Lots of turtles will ride the waves in to lay their eggs.

If you mark the nests, I will
come and pick up the eggs."
Benny gave a salute.
"Turtle Patrol is on duty!"

The Aldens headed down
the beach.
After a little while, Henry
found tracks in the sand.
They were hard to see,
but they led right to a nest!

Violet marked the spot with a flag.
Jessie put down rope to keep people away.
Benny inspected their work.
“Eggs-elent job, Turtle Patrol!”

The next nest was easy to find.
The turtle was still there!
People were gathered around.
In fact there was only one
person that did not seem
interested…

“Isn’t that Mr. Chatman?”
asked Violet.
He was sitting with a cooler by
a big van.
“Strange,” said Henry.
“I wonder why he isn’t helping.”

Jessie found the next set of
tracks.
This time it did not lead to
a turtle.
A big dog was sniffing the sand.
"Oh no," said Violet. "The eggs!"
A woman named Martina
ran up.
She pulled the dog away.
"I'm so sorry," she said.
"He got away from me."
"It's okay," said Henry, "but
please be careful next time."

Violet looked at the woman and dog.
Had she seen them the night before?

The Aldens finished their patrol.
They had marked three nests!
But when they saw Ranger
Thakur, she did not look happy.
She told them the eggs from
the nests were gone!
The Aldens searched each site.
They did not find any eggs.

But they did find two clues:
paw prints and tire tracks.
“Did an animal get them?”
asked Violet.
Ranger Thakur shook her head.
“Someone took these eggs.”

That night the Aldens talked
about their mystery.
Why would someone take
the eggs?
“Maybe they want pet turtles,”
said Henry.
“Or to sell them,” said Jessie.
“Whatever the reason, I’m sure
you will catch the culprit,” said
Grandfather.
Together the children came up
with a plan.

The next morning Henry, Jessie, Violet, and Benny went out on patrol.

This time when they found a turtle nest, Violet marked it with seashells.

Henry and Jessie put the flag and rope in a different spot.
"I get it," said Benny.
"If someone tries to dig at the flag, they won't find anything!"
They marked two nests with seashells.

After a little while, the Aldens
checked on the nests.
Their plan worked!
At the first flag, they found a
woman and a very big dog.
"Martina," said Violet. "Have
you been digging up our nests?"
"Digging up?" she asked.
"Oh no. I am training my dog
to sniff them out.
You see, I want to help the
rangers find more nests."
"That explains the paw prints,"
said Jessie.

The ranger joined them.
Martina's dog led the group
to the seashells Violet had
laid down.
Sure enough the nest was safe.

"But if you didn't take the eggs, who did?" asked Violet.
Henry had an idea.
He pointed to a white van down the beach.

“Do you know about the missing eggs?” the ranger asked Mr. Chatman.

At first the man looked mad. Then he sighed and nodded.

He went to his van and took
out his cooler.
Inside were all the missing eggs.
“It was your tire tracks we
found!” said Jessie.

Mr. Chatman explained.
His restaurant was not doing well.
He thought having sea turtles in his fish tank might bring in more people.
"That is not how you protect an endangered species," said Ranger Thakur.
"That's *dangerous* for them," said Benny.
"I see that now," said Mr. Chatman.
He handed over his Turtle Patrol badge.

A few days later the Aldens
woke up extra early.
They watched as the ranger
released baby sea turtles into
the ocean.
“They’re so small!” said Benny.

"I wish we could do more to
help them," said Violet.
"Maybe someday you will,"
said Ranger Thakur.
"But until then remember..."

"even the smallest thing can make a *big* difference."

Keep reading with The Boxcar Children®!

Henry, Jessie, Violet, and Benny used to live in a boxcar. Now they have adventures everywhere they go! Adapted from the beloved chapter book series, these early readers allow kids to begin reading with the stories that started it all.

HC 978-0-8075-0839-8 • US $12.99
PB 978-0-8075-0835-0 • US $4.99

HC 978-0-8075-7675-5 • US $12.99
PB 978-0-8075-7679-3 • US $4.99

HC 978-0-8075-9367-7 • US $12.99
PB 978-0-8075-9370-7 • US $4.99

HC 978-0-8075-5402-9 • US $12.99
PB 978-0-8075-5435-7 • US $4.99

HC 978-0-8075-5142-4 • US $12.99
PB 978-0-8075-5139-4 • US $4.99

HC 978-0-8075-0795-7 • US $12.99
PB 978-0-8075-0800-8 • US $4.99

GERTRUDE CHANDLER WARNER discovered when she was teaching that many readers who like an exciting story could find no books that were both easy and fun to read. She decided to try to meet this need, and her first book, *The Boxcar Children*, quickly proved she had succeeded.

Miss Warner drew on her own experiences to write the mystery. As a child she spent hours watching trains go by on the tracks opposite her family home. She often dreamed about what it would be like to set up housekeeping in a caboose or freight car—the situation the Alden children find themselves in.

While the mystery element is central to each of Miss Warner's books, she never thought of them as strictly juvenile mysteries. She liked to stress the Aldens' independence and resourcefulness and their solid New England devotion to using up and making do. The Aldens go about most of their adventures with as little adult supervision as possible—something else that delights young readers.

Miss Warner lived in Putnam, Connecticut, until her death in 1979. During her lifetime, she received hundreds of letters from girls and boys telling her how much they liked her books.